TWISTED TALES

STORIES OF IMAGINATION

Edited By Briony Kearney

First published in Great Britain in 2022 by:

Young Writers
Remus House
Coltsfoot Drive
Peterborough
PE2 9BF
Telephone: 01733 890066
Website: www.youngwriters.co.uk

Printed and bound in the UK by BookPrintingUK
Website: www.bookprintinguk.com
YB0501F

FOREWORD

Welcome, Reader!

Come into our lair, there's really nothing to fear. You may have heard bad things about the villains within these pages, but there's more to their stories than you might think...

For our latest competition, Twisted Tales, we challenged secondary school students to write a story in just 100 words that shows us another side to the traditional storybook villain. We asked them to look beyond the evil escapades and tell a story that shows a bad guy or girl in a new light. They were given optional story starters for a spark of inspiration, and could focus on their motivation, back story, or even what they get up to in their downtime!

And that's exactly what the authors in this anthology have done, giving us some unique new insights into those we usually consider the villain of the piece. The result is a thrilling and absorbing collection of stories written in a variety of styles, and it's a testament to the creativity of these young authors.

Here at Young Writers it's our aim to inspire the next generation and instill in them a love of creative writing, and what better way than to see their work in print? The imagination and skill within these pages are proof that we might just be achieving that aim! Congratulations to each of these fantastic authors.

CONTENTS

Abu Bakr Girls' School, Walsall

Annayah Hussain (13)	1
Fatima Adam (12)	2
Henna Begum (12)	3
Ruqayyah Shah (14)	4
Jana Younis (13)	5

Canterbury College, Canterbury

Phoebe Noble (17)	6
Maisie-Jane Hayes (17)	7
Rudy Weller (16)	8
Katie Gleed (17)	9
Haydn Mattin (16)	10
Tegan Weaving (16)	11
Emma West	12
Hollie Pearl (16)	13
Joe Arnold (17)	14
Owen Phipps (18)	15
Callum Spruce (17)	16
Jack Gridley (16)	17
Kayleigh Atherden (16)	18
Ben Hammond (17)	19
Dylan Robinson	20
Tom Marchant (16)	21
Imogen Zalech	22
Alfie Charles	23
Ibrahim Ahmadzai (17)	24
Eddie Theoff (16)	25
Callun Mannering	26
Keane Goldsmith (17)	27
Caylom Barnes (18)	28

Dragon School, Oxford

Margarethe Treeck (12)	29
Lottie Repp (11)	30
Mary Herrmann (11)	31
Jonathan Cohen Kadosh (12)	32

Jarrow School, Jarrow

Samuel Kinsey (12)	33
Aaron Earle (11)	34
Rosie-May Mccance	35
Chal Gilbert	36
Oliver McMillan	37
Noah Candlish	38

Sir John Leman High School, Beccles

Isobelle Thornton (12)	39
Evie-Mai Collins (12)	40
Daniel Peckham (12)	41
Harry Aspin (11)	42
Bella Crisp (12)	43
Benjamin Renicar (12)	44
Xavi Lee (11)	45
Kaila Smith (11)	46
Olivia Bice (11)	47
Sriram Prunthavan (11)	48
Harry Thompson (12)	49
Samuel Thompson (12)	50

The Gatwick School, Crawley

Vaidotas Pulokas (11)	51
Shanelle Terblanche (14)	52
Hamza Dawood (11)	53

Eliska Jobson (11)	54
Afqi Abdul-Salaam (11)	55
Josie Haste (11)	56
Adan Ali Khan (11)	57
Jessica Mary-Anne Cooke (13)	58
Hikma Riyas (13)	59
Elise Grace-Hills (15)	60
Sabina Basley (11)	61
Christopher Bourne (15)	62
Mariama Chaw (12)	63
Koray Caliskan (13)	64
Amy Paige Dolan (14)	65
Leon Pickersgill (15)	66
Kye Pizzey (14)	67
Ellie Kavanagh (11)	68
Emily Cowell (11)	69
Mia Hunt (11)	70
Halima Naveed (13)	71
Kye Price Nayee (12)	72
Luke Taylor (11)	73
Murphie Watson (13)	74
Gabriella Kate Nott (14)	75
George Peyton (11)	76
Aiyat Arif (14)	77
Benas Pajuodis (13)	78
Hana Ali (11)	79
Alexandra Harwood-Duffy (12)	80
Luke Damon (11)	81
Rose Waller (14)	82
Anuj Patel (13)	83
Robert Nicol (11)	84
Shaila Chandramohan (13)	85

Unity College, Towneley Holmes

Katie Swales (13)	86
Jessica Turbek (13)	87
Logan Scull (14)	88
Lacey Hargreaves	89
Ella Lewis (13)	90
Dalton Liversidge (14)	91
Nikita Golden (13)	92
Cooper Smith-Hands (13)	93
Eve Bainbridge (13)	94

Ruby Lambert (14)	95
Courtney O'Brien (12)	96
Nikita Goulding (13)	97
Jenson Thomas (14)	98
Courtenay Gallagher-Knowles (14)	99
Jessica Cullivan (13)	100
Evie Whitehead (13)	101
Grace Hargreaves (14)	102
Lacey Laycock (13)	103
Ellie Romao (14)	104
Aliceya Conroy (13)	105
Lacey Egerton (13)	106
Taiyan Burke (13)	107
Jake Kostilek (13)	108
Myles Blakey (13)	109
Liam Shaw (14)	110
William Lord (13)	111
Eva-Mai Morgan (13)	112
Owen Harris (13)	113
Bailey Canby (14)	114
Rowanne May-Jones (13)	115
Jack Butter-Haworth	116
Bedianur Sahin (11)	117
Khadijah Sarwar (14)	118
Shaania Alicia Shaw-Miah (13)	119
Tegan Dowling (14)	120
Alex Hughes (13)	121
Haaris Yaqub (15)	122
Lottie Norwood (13)	123
Isaac Ingham (13)	124
Emily Haworth (12)	125
Destiny Mannan	126
Alfie Johnson (13)	127
Ethan Turnbull (13)	128
Amelia Dean (14)	129
Owen Sharples (14)	130
Jaxon Ryder Cole (14)	131
Lola-Boe Robinson (14)	132
Evie Preston (13)	133
Annie Fort (14)	134
Jasper Cook (13)	135
Millie-Grace Edmondson (13)	136

Declan Collinge (13)   137
Rajeel Hashmi (14)   138
Lydia Wrathall (14)   139
Ruby Milliken (14)   140

THE
STORIES

ACATHARTOS

Finally, I was about to win. After all the effort, the time, the sacrificed souls, it was all paying off. I, Estella Acathartos, leader of the Yelidor Coven - nobody could stop me now, not even that brat, Morgana Agnos.

Abruptly, a hooded person burst through the oak doors. It was a lofty man and behind him stood Morgana. Her auburn hair swept across her shoulders and her cobalt eyes gazed at me. She darted towards me as angry as a raging bull. "Enough! This has to end now!" Morgana bellowed. "Dearie, this is just the beginning of the end."

Annayah Hussain (13)
Abu Bakr Girls' School, Walsall

1

THE WARRIOR OF THE FOREST

A part of the story...

Sara was an ordinary girl. But her life was soon to change...
She was off to school but realised she had left something!
So she went back to her house to get it. Sara realised that
she was now late for school so she took the short route.
Through the trees she went, she saw the school in the
distance but the distance between her and the school just
kept going further. She was confused, she didn't know what
was happening. Someone covered her face with a cloth... or
so she thought. Everything blurred out. What happened? we
wonder...

Fatima Adam (12)
Abu Bakr Girls' School, Walsall

THE MYSTERY HOUSE

Ryan was just a young boy when he moved house. When he arrived at the new place, he had a feeling that something was off, but he just brushed it off. A few days later, after moving into the new house, Ryan would always start feeling sick.

One evening, Ryan was getting ready to go out with his friends. When he looked in the mirror, he felt weird, but when he was about to leave, someone spoke. Ryan was confused and turned around to find a black figure in the mirror. The black figure spoke and said, "I want you!"

Henna Begum (12)
Abu Bakr Girls' School, Walsall

THE MURDERER

I did it to survive. There was no other choice...
I was there. The hairs on my neck stood up apprehensively
as footsteps approached me. I stood there, petrified. I had
never had this feeling before. I regretted this. He began to
laugh horrendously. I stared at him, as terrified as ever.
The feeling that everything I'd done in my life was useless. I
was useless. The clock stared at me. My sister had never
done anything, she was innocent. And I had become the
murderer because of him. It was all his fault.

Ruqayyah Shah (14)
Abu Bakr Girls' School, Walsall

THE MASKED MEN

I knew I shouldn't have trusted them from the start. Those masked men. That day, they saw me in the park, daring enough to be in the same park as them. They'd given me a bag to drop off at a building so horrible one may have thought it haunted.

I stared down at the trembling, helpless child, her soft whimpers echoing through my mind. This was for her own good. If I didn't kill her now, those masked men behind me would - but nastily. My hands shook as I held the sword high and pushed down. A scream.

Jana Younis (13)
Abu Bakr Girls' School, Walsall

THANOS LIVED HAPPILY EVER AFTER

Thanos leant back in his chair. "Finally I have succeeded," he sighed. Yet a heavy feeling tightened his chest. After wiping out half the population, Thanos had the space to breathe. *But was it worth it?* he wondered to himself. He'd lost everything he loved in the process.

At that thought, two young children came bursting through the doors. "Dad!" the youngest girl cried. "We found a snake."

Their mother, Pepper Potts, walked in holding the small corn snake. Thanos smiled, lifting the small child up in his arms carefully, kissed his wife and said, "Yes, this was worth it."

Phoebe Noble (17)
Canterbury College, Canterbury

AMELIA

Amelia, a young, beautiful, and bright woman, had just been given her mum's house due to her disappearance - the case was closed, presumed dead. She never really knew her mum, she was described as 'unstable'. The house was huge, with a big unkept and overgrown garden, beautiful nonetheless.
As Amelia opened the door, a disturbed and eerie presence washed over her with an ice-cold chill. She suddenly became overwhelmed with emotion, a sick, nauseous feeling building in her throat. Something was wrong with this house. Something evil, dangerous, unpredictable, lived here. She would soon find out.

Maisie-Jane Hayes (17)
Canterbury College, Canterbury

THE PIECE OF THE TRUTH

They fled, many fleeing to the neighbouring galaxy, thinking the slaughter would stop. They were wrong. Only one survived the Primordial, the last of the Precursors. Even now, as I looked upon his memories, I laughed as our timeless chorus filled their worlds, as they resorted to blowing their own stars and killing their own people.

The rightful successors were humanity but, even now, my hordes flooded their planet, feeding my energising compound mind. I found it amusing that this Lord Hood (was it?) thought he could stand against us. Us? Me? I had crushed an empire of trillions.

Rudy Weller (16)
Canterbury College, Canterbury

HAPPY AXEMAS

Every Christmas Eve, the Axemas killer has been hunting and killing anyone from the nice list out of spite! He was always on the naughty list for no reason until one Christmas Eve, he snapped.

The handle of Axemas' axe has snowflakes to represent his many victims. When he goes back to his cabin, every wall has axes with many snowflakes to represent the years of murder. Axemas gets a box wrapped in Christmas paper and puts his victims in the box. This goes to the family. When Christmas Day comes, Axemas will smile when he hears the screams.

Katie Gleed (17)
Canterbury College, Canterbury

THE PREDATOR

As the blinding sunlight broke through the trees, awakening me from my sleep, all was silent in the forest. I looked and listened out for any prey before setting out on a journey to find a meal. While I was hunting, I heard bushes rustling close by. I then saw a rabbit that hadn't noticed I was watching him.

Desperate for food, I tried to quietly sneak up behind the rabbit and attack them from behind. Eager for food, I wasn't paying attention to where I was stepping. I snapped a twig beneath my paws and the rabbit noticed me.

Haydn Mattin (16)
Canterbury College, Canterbury

LOKI THE MISUNDERSTOOD

I watched as my older brother struggled through the agonising pain. My heart was pounding fast as I was about to do something that would save my brother - but put the universe in danger. I handed over the Tessaract to Thanos, and the grimace on his face as he let go of Thor...
I sprinted faster than ever to him and held him. I felt something tighten around my neck, then I couldn't breathe. I watched the world slip into darkness and the last thing I saw was a tear roll down my brother's cheek. Then the darkness surrounded me.

Tegan Weaving (16)
Canterbury College, Canterbury

DR EVIL

There is a new villain in town, called Dr Evil. He bullies people and turns people into bullies to make a big army. He picks on the Flash. The Flash is a superhero, so turning him into a bully would be his best project yet.
He takes the Flash on and captures him. He then starts working on his brain and uses very weird scientific equipment - but suddenly the Flash wakes up! Dr Evil realises it's not working. The Flash and Dr Evil start to fight. *Pow! Pow! Pow!* The Flash wins this round and Dr Evil goes into hiding.

Emma West
Canterbury College, Canterbury

THE CHRISTMAS RIPPER

A smirk appeared on the mysterious figure by the woods as they were enveloped by darkness, much like the victims of their murders. It was a mystery as to why or who was doing it every century.

Crimson-red blood merged with the white, pure snow like good and evil merging together. The bodies of the Christmas Ripper lay motionless on the pillow of snow, almost looking at ease. Sliding the knife across their leather jacket, as if it would cleanse their sins.

The smell of smoke enveloped the nearby civilian's nostrils...

Hollie Pearl (16)
Canterbury College, Canterbury

THE VILLAINS

I still haven't forgotten that day when I tried to break into someone's car because I needed some money for Christmas. I only thought about stealing because I could get it and then sell it to make more money. But I didn't really care about the people's feelings, that was all I wanted to do. And try not to get caught. That's why I did it at night, cause people would be asleep so I didn't have to worry about it. The best thing I've stolen was a golden necklace because that's what I made the most from.

Joe Arnold (17)
Canterbury College, Canterbury

THE BANK JOB

As Joker is in the bank, his eyes start to light up as he sees the vault. There's a big bang, so many sparks and noises ringing in his head. Joker jumps in excitement as there is plenty of gold and money. He grabs the gold and money, filling his pockets until he hears a window smash.
Joker knows something is going on and feels a black figure behind him. There's a big bang, nothing to be said, Joker is knocked out cold on the floor. Batman stops the Joker and saves the day again. Joker is never seen again.

Owen Phipps (18)
Canterbury College, Canterbury

THE THING

I looked at an image of myself and then attacked. I ripped his head off and split him into two pieces. The blood went everywhere, it sprayed on the walls and dripped down them. As I let go of the destroyed body, a pool of blood spread around it.

I just walked back to the group and blended in, like a wolf in sheep's clothing, without them knowing a person even died. One of the humans would say, "Hey, Apollo, where have you been?"

I would tell them, "Oh, just to check the power."

Callum Spruce (17)
Canterbury College, Canterbury

BIG MAN JOKER

Joker woke up on a gorgeous Sunday. He was a very lonely villain, he didn't have any mates, let alone family, about. In his spare time, he got up to mischief. The one thing he cherished was his criminal side of life. He would rob people, steal top-of-the-range stuff, but when he tried to stop his addiction to being a criminal, he felt a certain way. Felt as if he was missing a certain thing. He just couldn't express his feelings. Four weeks later, his ex-girlfriend returned - he was nowhere to be seen.

Jack Gridley (16)
Canterbury College, Canterbury

A LOVE STORY FOR THE AGES

The sun hit my knife, making it shine like diamonds, but by the time school was over, my blade would be dull and the diamonds would turn to blood. I walked toward the building that was holding my victims.

He didn't understand that I was doing this for him. His black hair holding my heart hostage as I walked past him. My heart dropped as I walked through the school gates. My eyes caught my one true love with another girl. I drew my knife, I would paint the ground red to show him how much I love him.

Kayleigh Atherden (16)
Canterbury College, Canterbury

SCARECROW

I was a doctor trying to help people conquer their fears.
Now I am the one they fear. I was working on a chemical
compound to make people lose their fear, to be able to do
everything! It was working - then Batman and Robin just
had to disagree. I had to be quicker. Bombs full of fear gas
to help more people.

The plan was going well. I planted all the fear gas bombs
and they were ready to help the whole of Gotham City. Forty
years ago, and the bombs never went off. I'm still stuck in
Arkham Asylum!

Ben Hammond (17)
Canterbury College, Canterbury

PULLING THE SWITCH

I sat in a chair. I thought, *why did I get here?* I only murdered about 100 million people every week. I shouldn't need to be executed in this way. I needed to get out. I was the number one murderer.

What I did was right. I was trying to stop world hunger by killing lots of people. Then they captured me, just because I killed lots of people. I would get out. I just needed time. Why were they nearing the switch? Why were they pulling it? All I saw was darkness. Now where was I going?

Dylan Robinson
Canterbury College, Canterbury

THE STRUGGLES OF BEING DARTH VADER

Breathe. Breathe. Breathe. This mask makes it so hard. All I can hear is my own breath. Breathe. Again.

I hold my lightsaber close to my body. I am a panther ready to pounce. My son is nearby. I can feel him. Luke... Why does it always come to this? I am going to have to do something I regret to my son - but it is all part of what I have to do. And will be done for good reasons.

Why won't he just follow in his father's footsteps? I will have to swiftly kill my son, unfortunately.

Tom Marchant (16)
Canterbury College, Canterbury

THE PSYCHOPATH

I still haven't forgotten that time when that murderer went to prison for GBH and manslaughter. The jury was thinking *what was going through his mind?* The judge asked the murderer, "Why did you do these awful crimes?"
He gave a smug smile and looked down at the plain old floor. Who knew what was going on in that cold-hearted psycho mind of his...? The psycho showed no remorse when the judge gave him life in prison for manslaughter and GBH. No remorse at all.

Imogen Zalech
Canterbury College, Canterbury

THE DARK KNIGHT PROBLEM

Our story starts when I was free from this place. Before I decided to try to rule the world. I have had injuries from all different superheroes, from Batman too. I ended up killing him. I also have Superman, he is in a secret location, trapped so he can't get out. I know his weakness, it's so easy to defeat him. I don't know what the other villains were doing. All I know is, this man got shot in the head before he could tell us what had happened.

Alfie Charles
Canterbury College, Canterbury

THE MAGIC LAMP

I was going to win. I had served under the King for a long time. I wanted to take him down and marry his daughter. To do that, I needed the magic lamp. I wished to find the lamp and make myself the most powerful sorcerer in the world! I had found a boy in the marketplace, he was a thief. I took him to the Cave of Wonders to get the lamp. He betrayed me by taking the lamp! I decided to kill him. I would be the King of Agrabah!

Ibrahim Ahmadzai (17)
Canterbury College, Canterbury

SNAKE AND EAGLE

I was flying through the sky. Then I suddenly dived down because I saw a snake. I was very hungry. I needed something to eat and it was the only thing in miles to eat. The snake saw me, so it started to rapidly slither away from me. So I picked up the pace. Suddenly, he led me to another snake. I was surrounded, so I was trapped! I had no clue what to do. So I decided to attack one and grabbed it by the neck. I left him for dead.

Eddie Theoff (16)
Canterbury College, Canterbury

THE STORY OF A CAR THIEF

It was a cold night and I was searching around the streets for cars to steal. When I found one, I looked around for any cameras that could see me. Also to see if anyone could see me. When I saw no one was around, I proceeded to pick the car lock and then, when I was in the car, cut the wires to hot-wire it so I could start the vehicle. I started to drive off at speed, as I knew I could get a long time in prison for this.

Callun Mannering
Canterbury College, Canterbury

BOWSER

As I stood there, waiting for my opponent Mario, I was waiting with anticipation, waiting to see Mario come out of the small, green pipe. I jumped out and surprised Mario. I approached him and demanded he get out of my territory. He refused to leave my territory and he still was refusing to leave. He said he would leave once me and him had a fight to show who was more deserving. Okay with me. I was unstoppable.

Keane Goldsmith (17)

Canterbury College, Canterbury

GRIM REAPER LIFE

A body drops to the floor. I am relieved and move to the next victim, as I need souls to stay strong and to live. I breathe and wait for my next victim as, if I don't take their souls, the world will be overpopulated, cramped, and expensive. A lot of people see me as a villain but I am just a dark angel. I am just an angel in a dark place. I want to be a pure angel, like the others.

Caylom Barnes (18)
Canterbury College, Canterbury

WHY DID BEAUTY SLEEP?

I'm not the villain depicted in 'Sleeping Beauty'. Leah and I were besties when we both fell for Prince Hubert. He preferred Leah and married her. I took revenge by letting a savage dragon roam their kingdom.

Later, I killed it and gave King Stephan, Hubert's friend, an apology note for the King. Stephan burned it and said he killed the dragon! Wanting revenge, I cursed Leah's daughter, Aurora, so that Stephan's son, who was betrothed to Aurora, would probably die trying to rescue her. I only did it to get back at Stephan for framing me as the villain.

Margarethe Treeck (12)
Dragon School, Oxford

WHEN TIME HAS RUN OUT

My eyes were flickering, screaming in pain, my head, combusting with anger. If I hadn't done that, none of this would've happened. I was so close. They had to take it away. Lyra would've resolved it but the stupid kids kept running away.

My mind turned over. Did I really need to do that? The lab. The child. Dust.

It explained everything. I was so close. Snobby Mrs Coulter. That's why I'd needed Lyra. When I couldn't get her, I needed my own.

Blood rushed to my head...

Flood. Baby. Boat. Death. It wasn't worth it. It led to death...

Lottie Repp (11)
Dragon School, Oxford

THE CHIMAERA GOES VEGETARIAN

I had to make up for what I'd done. I'd killed so many, without realising it was wrong. I had to set things right. I plodded into the town square and stood on the podium and then I started talking.

"I'm sorry for killing all of those villagers. I didn't realise it was wrong. I've decided to go vegetarian - but only if you accept me and my fellow monsters. We were created by a malicious force and we only want acceptance."

I headed back to my cave, with the noises of deafening celebration in the background.

Mary Herrmann (11)
Dragon School, Oxford

HANSEL AND GRETEL: THE MOTHER'S STORY

I did it to survive. Scarcely enough bread for us! I shouldn't have left them near Mother's gingerbread house. At least they were fed and we'd also have food. I know it was wrong, but we were desperate!

We never heard of them again, probably eaten by Mother. Every day, playing in my head is the moment we threw them out. A few years ago, I peeped into Mother's house. I caught a glimpse of human remains lying in the oven. It sickened me.

In their memory, I started an orphanage. I have to make up for what I did.

Jonathan Cohen Kadosh (12)
Dragon School, Oxford

YELLOWSTONE

At 8pm at dusk in Yellowstone National Park, the scorpius rex assassinated the regional wildlife and elk, whilst the male baryonyx fished for food on the riverbank and the female baryonyx ate the salmon on the rocks. Suddenly, the scorpius rex launched for a bioluminescent parasaurolophus, murdering it then catapulting it towards the baryonyx creating a fight between the two species. At a nearby campsite, a helpless family camping screamed, "Help!"

Their camper was sent flying as the scorpius crashed into it. Luckily, Owen Grady came to the rescue, shooting the scorpius rex, leaving the baryonyx calm by the river.

Samuel Kinsey (12)
Jarrow School, Jarrow

A DAY OFF

I'm having a day off from work. Well, that's what I thought. Me, stuck at a birthday party. Great!

"I want a hug," screams a child.

Yes, finally, a child to start the party. He leaps for me as I stick my hand out and turn my boiling flamethrower on! "So, kids, where is the birthday girl?"

They all start running as I rip them away from their own bodies. Blood splatters on my face until I scream, "I thought you loved me!" I fall to the ground. Then comes the night. "Get ready, children..."

Aaron Earle (11)
Jarrow School, Jarrow

A

It was just like every day in Radley. I was hesitantly taking my medication when Wren came up to me.

"You have a visitor."

I looked behind him to see Spencer. I was scared, her and her friends always made me shiver.

"I know you did it!"

I knew I did but I didn't care. I was going to do worse to them. I thought to myself about what I did. I was proud of it, but Charles did that, not me. Charles was different. Cece was better. Cece had always been better than Charles. I'd got rid of Charles...

Rosie-May Mccance

Jarrow School, Jarrow

ILLUSIONS

As a young boy, my mother took me to the cinema and I loved it! The great CGI was mind-boggling, and how the directors got what they wanted was even better.
When I wasn't doing anything, I would learn to do illusions and CGI. Then, when I went to Baxron College, I learnt about psychology and how to brainwash animals and people. Nowadays, I hunt people, make them think they're seeing things. Then I kidnap them and make them one of my many minions. Eventually, I will have an army big enough to take over the world!

Chal Gilbert
Jarrow School, Jarrow

A HOLIDAY

I'm taking a day off from taking spirits to the afterlife. My job as the grim reaper is stressful, so a holiday is my only choice.

As I'm taking a walk in the forest, I hear a yelp. A wolf is trapped under an enormous tree branch, so I free him. I continue my walk and find a waterfall. As I sit down, I hear a deafening scream.

I spin around instantly and there stands an old lady. I quickly try to calm her but she runs, slips, falls. She lets out a scream and it's over. My holiday's over.

Oliver McMillan
Jarrow School, Jarrow

WHO IS THE REAL VILLAIN?

I could sense the victory in the air. I looked into my brother's eyes, as I knew we would defeat him. He was about to slash me with his deadly lightning bolt, however, I sucked the life and power from his soul.

I could see, in my mind, the prize. I would win the throne of Mount Olympus. I was fighting for this throne with all I could offer.

As I entered the heavens, I heard the deathly whistle. I turned my head to see the son of Zeus, Hercules. "Hercules, who is the villain now?"

Noah Candlish
Jarrow School, Jarrow

THE DECISION

I vividly remember the day I was released from my virtual imprisonment. "Come get my riches," I taunted in chat. "It's buried inside the gloomiest corner of my fortress."
I saw them from quite a distance, vibrantly coloured and ambitious. They crept inside and peered at the blood-stained painting and wondered if they'd be next. Wandering on, curious as ever, longing to find my treasure. The door creaked open to the room. I suddenly appeared, gun in hand.
Would I? I had to. My hands shook and my palms sweated. If I had shot, they'd replace me. I'm sorry... *bang!*

Isobelle Thornton (12)
Sir John Leman High School, Beccles

GASTON'S ORIGIN

Sobs erupted from his chest. She'd left him. Him and everyone else. Today was her funeral. Tears streamed down people's faces. His wife, Rose, had disappeared forever. Down the cliff, she'd tumbled. According to the police. Her corpse, lifeless, no one had come to her aid. She just wanted to pick flowers for their new house. But now the house was dead inside, a building with no soul. His heart was shattered, broken into pieces.

When he thought things couldn't get any worse, he saw a girl who looked just like Rose... and he knew he had to get her.

Evie-Mai Collins (12)
Sir John Leman High School, Beccles

IT'S HARD BEING A BEE

It's very hard being special. Everyone gets jealous. I do a very important job, I collect pollen and I pollinate your flowers in summer, day in, day out. Humans are killing us because they annoy us. We die after using our sting. It can't grow back like our relatives' sting can. Every day we live in worry. Will I die? Will it be our last? Our lives are being destroyed and my species faces extinction.

Please do something. Please help us, or otherwise we will die out and you won't have flowers or honey. Save us, please, we need help!

Daniel Peckham (12)
Sir John Leman High School, Beccles

THE AMBUSH

Chewing through the floorboards, I was that day. It was a normal thing for us rats, only way we could get food. Obviously, the humans hated it and many of our brothers died in their rat traps. But today was the day we would strike back. This heist would go down in history. Right into first place in the book of golden cheese. We would be worshipped as gods.

Bang! The sound of a semi-automatic assault rifle rang. The children were screaming, families were scrambling, and my vision, it was failing. I could feel and touch the light...

Harry Aspin (11)
Sir John Leman High School, Beccles

WHY ME?

Everyone always judges the villain. Always the hero. What if the villain wanted to be the hero for once? All these centuries and it's always a competition and he is the chosen one for success. There will be revenge.

As I stumble toward his house, suddenly, I hear a crunch. What I was about to witness was utterly horrifying. As I glance down, all I can see is his name badge. As I sigh with relief, thinking that it is just a rumour, I see his murderer writing in a red substance: *Better luck next time.* Who is this man?

Bella Crisp (12)
Sir John Leman High School, Beccles

MY HITMAN LIFE

People hate on me just because of my questionable occupation. My previous history in jail leaves me no choice but to pursue being a hitman. I don't gruesomely shoot them, I just slowly put them to sleep and they don't feel a thing! My six-year-old son at home needs to be fed and my skills in combat make me the perfect fit.

This one client paid me a large sum to make their spouse barbarically perish and I agreed! Apart from one thing: I said I would shoot them but I didn't. I just smothered them as usual.

Benjamin Renicar (12)
Sir John Leman High School, Beccles

DEATH WONDERS

While I sit and watch them from my place in the sky, I wonder what it's like being human. After all, I'm death itself. Choosing when it is people's time to leave this world and I have no contact with Earth at all.

It gets lonely up here. I wonder if I could bring a human up here to chat with, but it seems impossible. I also wonder what food tastes like. I've never eaten in my life. I haven't done a lot of things in my lifetime, in fact, I don't have a lifetime. I'm Death. I never die.

Xavi Lee (11)
Sir John Leman High School, Beccles

SPIDERS LIKE ME

They say we're scary, they say we should be dead, but without us, there would be flies all around! It's not our fault we crawl on the ground. Spiders. We go out for a minute, back to my home, I climb on. But I fall because some careless human has stomped it, gone! Spiders. The humans are like giants. Why are they scared of us? We only want to hug them, it's only usually on the bus! Spiders. We go in nice warm crannies, it's ever so dark. We are only at your granny's, or we are at the park.

Kaila Smith (11)
Sir John Leman High School, Beccles

BARNEY THE SPIDER

Today, I found a nice cosy home called a bus. It was much cosier than outside. I decided to lay my head on the windowsill on the bus. It was a nice journey.

Then I realised that there was a human next to me. *Yay! A new friend!* I thought. She looked quite relaxed, listening to music. I decided to say hello. I climbed up her shoulder and she turned to me... She looked mortified. Then she scooped me up with a mask and put me back, keeping her distance before getting off. So much for a new friend!

Olivia Bice (11)
Sir John Leman High School, Beccles

CELABI THE SPIDER

It's so hard to be a spider. All these dumb humans try to kill me. All I want to do is steal their food and live in their ceiling corners - and I even eat the flies that taste horrible to them. Ungrateful fools.

Oh. Oh no. I have run out of food. That means I must get some food from them. It's time. To the food basket, upsidedown, I crept. My silk longer as time passes. Sweat drops. I've got it.

Oh no! The human's come and with a ruler. I accept fate and close my eyes.

Sriram Prunthavan (11)
Sir John Leman High School, Beccles

THE REVENGE OF THE WASP

It's so hard to be a wasp. Wasps are just little and cute but people only see the bad side of us. We just want somewhere to live. Humans just assume that we want to sting them. It's nice and warm in people's houses - but one human, one human trapped my friend in a cup and suffocated him. That day, I knew revenge was the only option. I went into their house, made them aware that I was there. I struck when they were asleep. I stung all of them. It was great to see misery in the house.

Harry Thompson (12)
Sir John Leman High School, Beccles

IT'S A WASP LIFE

My life is so hard. Always trying to harvest pollen and I need to provide for my kids. I just want to live a normal life without getting swatted by humans. One day, I will get killed like my family and, just like me, they will have to provide for their family or themselves. I only have a few more days to wait and my wife's offspring will be ready and I will finally have hundreds of other wasps by my side. And I will be victorious as I take revenge on the humans that always hurt me.

Samuel Thompson (12)
Sir John Leman High School, Beccles

THE HEAVEN'S BETRAYAL

A thundercloud appeared in the distance. It seemed like an angel had arrived. Next second, it was in front of me. "Who are you?" I asked.

"Lucifer," he replied in a loud, deep voice.

"Why are you here?"

"To take over the world. And I want you to join me."

"Why? Why me?"

"My power and your intelligence can rule anyone, even God."

"What if I don't?"

"I will enslave you and steal your intelligence."

My heart dropped. Shivers crawled through my body.

"Just think about it. Think how powerful we can be... Well, do you accept this offer?"

Vaidotas Pulokas (11)
The Gatwick School, Crawley

THE MISUNDERSTOOD BAKER

A plump lady waddled toward the stove which was made of gingerbread, as was the rest of the house. Margaret finally released a suffocating sigh as her eyes led her to two framed photos on the sweet-covered wall. A bubble of emotions popped above her and sadness overtook her. The liquorice decorated frames revealed two gleeful children - Margaret's children. "I miss you two," she commented cheerlessly.

To occupy her lonely mind, Margaret decorated her house with sugary treats. The tantalising smell of fresh gingerbread beckoned two young children, Hansel and Gretel, to come in. Finally, Margaret was not alone.

Shanelle Terblanche (14)
The Gatwick School, Crawley

VENOM: LET THERE BE CARNAGE

After sending the dangerous Riot back to space, Eddie and Venom decided to go home and sleep. The next day, Eddie went to go and get some breakfast.

"Can I have some breakfast?" said Venom.

"Okay, just remember: when you live in my body, you live by my rules."

"How dare you!" shouted Venom. He bonked Eddie on the nose.

"What was that for?" said Eddie worriedly.

"You're a loser, Eddie."

They decided to go into the city and they saw this serial killer called Cletus Kasady. Then, all of a sudden, he transformed into Carnage.

"Oh, no..."

Hamza Dawood (11)
The Gatwick School, Crawley

A CHANGE OF GODMOTHER

Glass shattered everywhere. The fairy godmother grinned in the shadows as she watched the rigged shoes blow up. Cinderella fell to the ground and the Prince caught up with her.

"Are you okay?" he asked kindly.

The fairy godmother grimaced and waved her hands. Suddenly, the Prince's eyes went red and he picked up a piece of shattered glass. He then drew the piece down, cracking Cinderella's head in half. Blood spilt all over his new suit as a dead Cinderella lay on the steps.

The fairy godmother had gotten her wish - revenge. Revenge on, in fact, Cinderella's own mother.

Eliska Jobson (11)
The Gatwick School, Crawley

GRENDEL AND BATMAN

Grendel was known as a ferocious, bloodthirsty monster who just wanted to suck the life out of children that played in the meadows. Grendel came out of his cave that was hidden away with cobwebs.

Then the mighty hero came onto the battlefield. "Bats," Batman said. Bats came from huge numbers, like hailstones falling from the air. Crowds came in huge numbers. Batman attacked Grendel from all sides.

The monster was feeling tremendous pain, but that was good. The battlefield was a huge, bloody mess. Blood soaked the dirt path. But the fighting continued with Grendel and Batman in agony.

Afqi Abdul-Salaam (11)
The Gatwick School, Crawley

TREASURE ORGANS

Dark days. Late nights. The daughter of the family lies on the sofa with her mother. Since Chris, her father, was arrested.

Chris was a bad guy, he did many disturbing murders. The worst villain. The most wanted villain. The most evil villain. In 1978 he murdered a family of three, then spread their organs around random destinations. This murder was named 'Treasure Organs'.

Chris may have been named as bad, but we can't forget his caring side. He helped out charities and was a caring father. He may have done some bad stuff, but everyone has a good side...

Josie Haste (11)
The Gatwick School, Crawley

THE SOUL SNATCHER

Clunk! Clunk! Clank! Clunk! Aagh!
I woke up. I walked to my parents' room. "Mum, Dad?" I walked in. Their eyes were pitch-black! It was like something sucked their souls. *Whoosh! Clunk!* I heard the window close - whatever it was, was still in this room...
I dashed to the bathroom, locked it, and took out a massive broom. I camped in there for an hour and I kept hearing strange, faint groans. Two hours later, it stopped.
I walked downstairs. I heard some sounds in the kitchen. I ran in. Wait, it was my brother, Jake, dead.

Adan Ali Khan (11)
The Gatwick School, Crawley

HEADLESS

I still haven't forgotten what I saw. My best friend's body lying on the ground. Except that she wasn't dead. Her blue orbs stared into mine, pleading for help. Except I was glued to the ground, shaking.

My boyfriend stood over her, ripping flesh from her body, a pool of crimson blood at her feet. She screamed in pain. He ripped off her head and this time I screamed. My friend and boyfriend's heads simultaneously snapped toward me, their eyes boring into mine. My boyfriend stood up and ambled toward me. He looked dead and extremely hungry. Oh god.

Jessica Mary-Anne Cooke (13)
The Gatwick School, Crawley

SOULS OF THE REAPER

She had five minutes, just five. Darkness engulfed the shack, her frame towering above the furniture. The man was ghost-faced, the woman staring down at him pityingly.

She had lived before the making of time, yet she still found humans fascinating. Mourning for each soul she stole. Reaching out, she let the wisp of white gas fly into her bag. A collection of the dead, delivered to the afterlife each night at the dead of dawn.

As the woman walked out of the shack, her cloak revealing nothing but her nimble fingers, the faint sound of whispers filled the air.

Hikma Riyas (13)
The Gatwick School, Crawley

REVENGEFUL RIDDLE

I did it for a reason. They changed my name. Sometimes, wizards and witches hate the thought of me - but I was trying to make everything right.

It happened one night in the dungeons. I was on my way to the dorms while the school started closing for the night. I overheard the distant whispers in the corridors, Hagrid and Dumbledore were discussing the whereabouts of a student. I heard my name.

The flames lightened in the corridor with such fear, engulfing the candles inside. My inner anger and revenge struck. They wanted rid of me. Rid of Thomas Riddle.

Elise Grace-Hills (15)
The Gatwick School, Crawley

THE SURPRISING PLOT TWIST

One fatal day, an unforgettable fight against Hawk Moth took place. He had abandoned the lair as the two so-called heroes broke in. Hawk Moth retreated to the Eiffel Tower. Once arriving, he fell to his knees. He could hardly move. He watched as the heroes got closer. Hawk Moth built up all the strength left and ran. He landed on his feet and ran behind a house. He whispered in despair, "I have to stop here."

Suddenly, the heroes found him. He was taken away by the police. He knew what he must do. He saw Ladybug's grim expression.

Sabina Basley (11)
The Gatwick School, Crawley

THE SUFFERING

He stood there over the body of his kinsman.
"The pain I felt that day was immense, the tears wouldn't stop." He paused. "I shall make this world feel the same pain that I felt. This war will end as only those who know true pain truly appreciate peace."
Through all the years, nobody would help a small child who was starving. That was the truth of this reality and society. "So, to fix that, I shall destroy this society and start a new world. Fire the hell cannons and make this world burn. Now, you die."

Christopher Bourne (15)
The Gatwick School, Crawley

MY DEAD MOTHER

I still haven't forgotten the day I found my mother dead. I was walking through the woods alone, getting away from life. It was dark. You could see the city's streetlights in the distance. It was only the moon lighting up the forest.

I walked further and started seeing flies and dead animals. They'd been chewed to death. I was frightened but carried on walking. I saw some legs coming out of the bushes. I looked behind them and saw my dead mother.

I screamed and looked around. There was a pair of yellow eyes just staring at me.

Mariama Chaw (12)
The Gatwick School, Crawley

THE CAMPSITE

It was a dark winter's night. The cafeteria lights were flickering. The campsite was dark and eerie. Suddenly, as I was about to eat, the door got smashed open. It was a werewolf. The same one that was described last night around the fire. It barged through, destroyed everything in its path. It ran straight toward Jack. It started growling loudly before pouncing on top of him and ripping the flesh off his body. People screamed like it was the end of the world. Blood squirted in all directions. The wolf leapt toward me quickly. Then I woke up.

Koray Caliskan (13)
The Gatwick School, Crawley

DEATH IS I

The life drains from whatever I lay my finger upon. Any people who I try to befriend dodge the path I stroll, yet I once had a friend.

What is so dreadful about death? My blood boils with rage, yet my heart sobs with compassion. My once best friend, my now enemy. The one I couldn't kill. The one I didn't want to kill.

Blinding, beaming and bright, the soul of every party. Lurking deep in the shadow of this great light, stands me. The sea of jealously engulfs my existence but it won't defeat me, won't drown my screams.

Amy Paige Dolan (14)
The Gatwick School, Crawley

THE BIG BAD WOLF AND LITTLE RED RIDING HOOD

Once, there was a family of two. There was a granddaughter and grandmother. They had a little house in the forest, it was surrounded by lots of different trees and shrubs.

Later that day, the young girl walked down to the forest to collect some apples. I sneakily spied on her to gobble her up once she'd collected enough apples in her basket. Ten minutes later, the young girl made her way home. I launched myself from the highest branch and chased her. She tripped over a broken log on the ground and I gobbled her up, basket and all.

Leon Pickersgill (15)
The Gatwick School, Crawley

HOOK'S LOSS

"I failed," said James. "I failed to stop him, to protect the children."

As the Captain fell from the mast, all of the crew looked up in horror, talking to the world about how the world was doomed. Peter had won. Hook had lost. The crew waited for the crocodile to snap its jaws shut with a loud crunch, knowing what was coming next. Knowing what Peter would do to both the children and the world. They also knew what came next for them. Captain Hook had failed and was killed and they were all going to walk the plank.

Kye Pizzey (14)
The Gatwick School, Crawley

A 13-YEAR-OLD WITH TWO LIVES

A thirteen-year-old murderer with two lives. Everyone thought she was a sweet girl but it drove her mad. During her classes at school, no one knew what she was thinking. Maybe plotting how she would kill her classmates. Jennifer was her victim today. She was shy, all her victims were. At the end of school, the thirteen-year-old followed her. As she was reaching for the knife, she thought, *why do I do this?* She stopped reaching for the knife. It was to hide the pain. She did this to forget about home. She did this to survive.

Ellie Kavanagh (11)
The Gatwick School, Crawley

EVIL-RELLA (TWISTED CINDERELLA)

I woke up in the dead of night with a jump. My sister, Clorinda, heard it too. We gave each other a look as to say, *let's go investigate*. We crept down the long staircase, trying to not make a sound.

A strange, green light illuminated the ballroom. We opened the door a little, to let us peek through. What we saw shocked us. Cinderella stood in the middle of the room, chanting some weird spell... A strange figure stood in the far corner, facing Cindy. The Prince! What was she doing to the Prince? We had to investigate!

Emily Cowell (11)

The Gatwick School, Crawley

DEATH'S FRIEND

Death was mean and cruel. He took people's breath away and stopped their hearts. But all he was, was lonely. He wanted friends. Trapped in a large, dark box, alone for what seemed like forever. He was scared, unable to see, lost. But for how long? He believed forever that he was punished for something he had done, something he was unable to remember. Until there was light! Far away, but there was definitely light. A speck. He floated over as quick as he could until he could make out the silhouette of a man. Good, finally, a friend.

Mia Hunt (11)
The Gatwick School, Crawley

CEREBRAL MATTER

I never really belonged here. I was different from my foster family. My family were all kind, weak, and forgiving. I was the complete opposite, brave and strong.

But something happened to me yesterday night when two burglars came to rob our house. My parents weren't home, they were on vacation, and my siblings couldn't do anything because they were weak. So I got up and tried to hit one of them on the head but I missed. Then they tried to grab me, but somehow I was controlling them with my brain! So now I was in control!

Halima Naveed (13)
The Gatwick School, Crawley

THE STORY OF BORIS JOHNSON

I did it to survive. I had to become Prime Minister to survive. I needed people to protect me. The first thing I thought about being Prime Minister - I hate being Prime Minister. People know me as Boris Johnson.

I am only here because I'm getting chased by spies because they want my money. They're killing lots of my people. I thought it was strange, if they won't kill me, why are they killing my people? But it turned out, suddenly, all the people at my mansion were trying to kill me. They were teaming up on me.

Kye Price Nayee (12)
The Gatwick School, Crawley

THE DARK NIGHT

It was a dark, dark night when Venom came out to cause some destruction. He wanted to kill and have lots of fun. I heard a loud *bang!* Another *boom!* This was the sixth one. Where was Spider-Man? We needed him. The whole city was falling apart. What about the city's people? They were all going to die.

Look! It was Spider-Man. He was killing Venom. Get him Spider-Man! Kill him! Kill him! Push him out of the city. Thank you, Spider-Man. You saved the whole city. You are the biggest, biggest hero.

Luke Taylor (11)
The Gatwick School, Crawley

THE RIPPER

Then dropped the first victim of Jack the Ripper. Look at that. That reminds me of my mother. All over men, all day, every day. It makes me sick to my stomach, watching them have fun while people like me have to sit in the shadows of the men they pleasure.

I'm going to put an end to prostitutes - like my mother, who abandon their kin and become selfish. Do I feel guilty? No, not even when the blood is dripping off my hands after I've killed my victims. After I'm finished, this world will be much better.

Murphie Watson (13)
The Gatwick School, Crawley

FIONA'S TALE

As Fiona woke in her bed, she saw Lord Farquaad unbearably leaning over her. He praised how her body looked, but in the mirror she still saw an ogre. Again, he praised her beauty. She raged over to her mirror and smashed it into pieces, to find Lord Farquaad disgusted, in horror.

She ran out of her castle, crying with despair, as a storm emerged around her. It vacuumed everyone and everything in. The storm made the bodies fall to the ground as Fiona sucked their souls. She wandered back to find her body on her bed.

Gabriella Kate Nott (14)
The Gatwick School, Crawley

SYMBIOTE BATTLE

Bang! The door smashed open. I woke up in shock. I ran downstairs to see a man running around the room like a dog. "What on Earth are you doing?" I said.

The man came to me. "We have no time. Symbiotes are attacking the city, we are all doomed. And if they get people then it is the next level of trouble. It's up to you to save the world. All you need to do is fight the Symbiote King. Here, have this." He pulled out a case with armour as tough as steel.

"I'm in."

George Peyton (11)
The Gatwick School, Crawley

THE NIGHT I DIED

My plan was failing. I was caught. The police had found me. I was running for my life. It was midnight, the rain was rushing down and the police sirens were loud. The dead bodies were found, but how? I was confused, thoughts were racing through my mind.

I didn't know whether to pay attention to my thoughts or the fact that the police were after me. I crossed the road and a car crashed into me. I quickly got up. Someone came out of the car, they were all in black. It was an undercover officer. I was caught!

Aiyat Arif (14)
The Gatwick School, Crawley

JUST A MINUTE AGO

Finally, I was about to win. The five years I spent trying to kill Dwayne Goliath had ended. He killed my father, I had to get revenge!

Dwayne killed him in cold blood. He had blood dripping from every corner of his body, but I still couldn't do it. Why, why, why? Just a minute ago, all I had on my mind was killing this disgusting man. But now I was feeling guilty - not just that, I was feeling sympathetic for him!

Why couldn't I bring myself to do it? I wanted to kill him but I couldn't.

Benas Pajuodis (13)
The Gatwick School, Crawley

THE RED WOLF AND THE EVIL GRANNY

A long time ago, in the gloomy forest, was the time when Red Riding Hood and her grandma were in danger. But the wolf was not going anywhere, even though they escaped. The old grandma was going to take revenge and this was the day the wolf would never forget.

One day, the old lady was planning the best death for the beast. She studied witchcraft and learned Kung-Fu. Once she stopped, she would show Little Red Riding Hood. And then they were ready. They were coming for him - and he had no idea...

Hana Ali (11)
The Gatwick School, Crawley

I DID IT FOR HER

Finally, he was dead. Many would think of me as a murderer but the way I saw it was, the fact that I saw this baby's future and it wasn't a bright one. I was about to lose everything, my children, my home, everything. Just to protect her. She must hate me, but I couldn't let her life end that way.

Someone was behind me. There I was, hell. Just for protecting my child. But I knew what her brother was going to do. I had to. And yet, to this day, I was still known as a murderer.

Alexandra Harwood-Duffy (12)
The Gatwick School, Crawley

THE EVIL SQUIRREL

It all started the day I felt darkness consume me. It was an evil day of pain. As I am the evil squirrel. That day, the day the humans lost control, was the day I ruled the world. Now, I have more power than ever. I have the humans at my command, at the edge of my finger.

I never meant to do this. It was so painful. The injections, mind control... but I broke free. Stronger than ever. And I struck back. Now, I use the machine on humans to make them feel my suffering. I want redemption.

Luke Damon (11)
The Gatwick School, Crawley

THE WRONG IDEA

I did it to survive... The hacker knew my exact location which meant I had to move fast. I quickly packed some stuff and ran out the front door. I was thinking to go to a friend's house, but realised that was too risky so I just went to the shops for some food. In my head, I knew that game was the wrong idea to do.

I was starting to debate what to do. There was one thing I could do: run into the forest. Everyone was speaking about how people had gone missing, but I had no choice.

Rose Waller (14)
The Gatwick School, Crawley

THE STRANGE CHRISTMAS

He was my best friend, he was my everything. Let me explain. It was a cold winter day and me and John had decided to look at our presents. He said they were at his house. I was confused at first why my presents were there, but then I agreed to go.

As we walked in, it was dark. It smelt really bad. I didn't know why my presents were there. Or were they? Suddenly, the light turned on and these odd-looking people (Spike and Joe) ran after me. And then I realised, John had set me up.

Anuj Patel (13)
The Gatwick School, Crawley

THE JOKER AND BATMAN

One day, the Joker was on a nice walk to the park to rob it. Then Batman stopped him and threw him in jail. Two days later, the Joker escaped to find Batman. He turned out to be hypnotised by Lex Luthor. So they went to find Luthor to confront him.

He said Joker was lying. He knew that he was lying himself. The Joker made a plan to capture him. He went to the pool tunnel and when Lex came, he pulled him underwater and threw him in jail. And then they all had some tea.

Robert Nicol (11)
The Gatwick School, Crawley

HAUNTED LOVE

I did it to survive. I only did it because he was going to kill me. It all started when I was at home with my husband. Things were all fine until he started acting fishy.

One day, he was in the bedroom and I checked and he text someone saying he wanted to kill me. I packed my stuff. He saw me and asked what was happening. So I suddenly ran. He got me and tried killing me. I quickly thought I would fake my death. So I played dead. He saw and ran. I was then gone...

Shaila Chandramohan (13)

The Gatwick School, Crawley

DON'T LIE TO A VAMPIRE

"I still haven't forgotten what your great-grandad did to me!" he shouted.

"I... I don't know what you are on about," the boy cried.

"Yes you do," he said. "You know everything." He had been locked up by this family for years. Five centuries exactly. Now he'd decided to kill all of them for the next five centuries. He'd killed over fifty people from this family, boys and girls.

"Tell me where it is. What is the code?"

"It's in there," the boy cried.

"Thanks, that wasn't so hard was it? Now you're dead."

Katie Swales (13)

Unity College, Towneley Holmes

THE ORIGIN

"Mummy! Where are they taking me? Save me, save me!" Oliver gave out an ear-rattling shriek. Desperately holding onto his mother, kicking his tiny legs about rapidly.

Knowing whatever Oliver protested with wasn't working, she replied frantically, "I won't let go of you, ever. I love you, Oli."

Violently, the men ceased his flailing arms in an attempt to pull him off his weeping mother. Unfortunately, her once elegant dress was now torn drastically at the hips and had lost its beauty in an instant. Oliver was gone, destructively, her heart had been shattered into a million pieces.

Jessica Turbek (13)
Unity College, Towneley Holmes

THE MIST

Mist trailed him down the dark corridor. A large oak door was visible up ahead. Swinging open, the large door released the aura of the darkened room onto him. Looking over to the right, a row of pillars followed down the wall, masking the wall in a striped darkness.

Quickly, he rushed over toward their direction while the pursuing mist entered the room intrusively. Sweating profusely in fear, he lay silent but the light *thud* grew in volume. A growl made its presence known, with the accompanying footsteps stopping. Feral dogs released themselves from the mist.

"Oh no..." he muttered.

Logan Scull (14)
Unity College, Towneley Holmes

WE RULE

I still haven't forgotten everything that they made us do. It's time to get revenge. We have been slaving over these humans. Soon we will rule the world. These humans don't know what's in store for them. I plan for me to reign and take over.

The humans are trying everything to stop us. Dead. That's two humans down. Bones everywhere for dinner later. Blood scattered everywhere. Guts dripping from animals' mouths. People running faster than lightning. Meanwhile, creatures, animals, were everywhere, killing the population. Soon, only a few will be left. And we will have victory.

Lacey Hargreaves

Unity College, Towneley Holmes

IT'S JUST A DREAM

Startled by the creeping fear that someone was there, in my room, I tried to wake myself. Slumber seized me like early morning mist to the ground. I was trapped. In and out of consciousness, smothered by piercing screams. Piercing cries fueled a galvanising fear inside me.

Was I losing my sanity? I firmly shut my eyes, diligently trying to squeeze the deafening cries from my mind. *It's just a dream*, I thought, trying to relax myself. Finally calm, I started to fall into a trance-like state. Suddenly, hundreds of horrifying screams violently reeled me back into the torturous trap.

Ella Lewis (13)
Unity College, Towneley Holmes

THE CHILDREN'S HOME

Squealing, the gate opened for the notorious explorer. He had just entered the abandoned children's home. Slowly, he opened the rotting door and gazed at all the bright, neon graffiti. Gathering his senses and wits, he trembled forward slowly. The door closed even though there was no wind. *Crack!* An unwashed child sprinted loudly across the hallway. Finding there was blood on the walls, he dashed through the seemingly endless hallway. He tried to reach the exit. Appearing out of nowhere, the crooked, unloved child stopped him in his tracks to carefully dismember the explorer.

Dalton Liversidge (14)
Unity College, Towneley Holmes

FLAMING ANGER

Blue fire burned brighter than lightning. Other children had gorgeously tanned arms and faces with curly or straight locks. Cute button noses with cheeky smiles. But Hades was a different child. His cracked, pale skin was battered and bruised like a broken pinata - but with no laughing, sweets, joy. Just a rotten personality with plenty of death and jealousy.

Hades really didn't mean for it to be like that. All he wanted was a friend. Or maybe a new family. Ever since his older brother got into trouble, they had blamed Hades for their failures. The 'brothers' were no more.

Nikita Golden (13)
Unity College, Towneley Holmes

HAUNTED FLAT

In a cold town, a woman lived with her father. She'd newly moved there with him in the late spring to the so-called haunted apartment. The second morning, her father was dead. "This is all a coincidence, it's not possible," she muttered.

The night before the funeral, a creepy figure appeared in her dreams, glaring with wide eyes and an item at hand. A knife, maybe. The morning after the funeral, she came home to wide open doors. She noticed the knives were gone then, suddenly, *thud!*

That's all she remembered after waking up in the abandoned asylum.

Cooper Smith-Hands (13)

Unity College, Towneley Holmes

TRAPPED

Mist hovered through the ghost-like sky as the pungent smell of chemicals swiftly spread through the air. In the depths of the forest, lurked a poor, under-nourished soul, running through the decaying wildlife. Trapped, with no possible way of getting out, she thought she'd left this lost, deserted place, but no.

The tiredness caused by running took over her body as she roughly dropped to the ground, barely able to open her eyes. She lay there, not knowing what would happen next. A power light source struck her eyes, lively flowers all around. Was this a new start for her?

Eve Bainbridge (13)
Unity College, Towneley Holmes

BERTHA'S LIES

Patiently, I waited. Sat still on my chair. I couldn't let her think I was the one using her but I had no other choice than to kill her.

Bursting open the door, "It was you all along!" she screamed in temper.

"It was for the best. I didn't mean for you to find out like this," I said as I tried to put on a sad face.

"I trusted you, Bertha, I thought our friendship was strong," she said.

"Things change. No one will believe you anyway," I said.

"But don't worry, it'll be over soon," I said smugly.

Ruby Lambert (14)

Unity College, Towneley Holmes

MAGIC MISTAKE

They could only blame themselves. It was all their fault. A childhood full of neglect. I was invisible. Now I would make myself seen. They'd see the monster they created. I would make sure of it. My perfect sister would see too. I'd made my decision, there was no turning back.

With my sceptre at hand, I made my way to the academy. As I expected, my sister was waiting. A spark of good magic flew from her hand. "The academy hasn't taught you enough," I laughed.

"Just enough to get rid of you." *Boom!* Magic flew. She was dead!

Courtney O'Brien (12)
Unity College, Towneley Holmes

THE MAN OF ACT

The man. Always very quiet but he may come across as aggressive. He always dressed elegant, ready for business, but the ladies thought different. He was very attractive. He had bright, electric-blue eyes that caught your attention before anything else did. What lay behind the attractiveness was a monster.

The guilt haunted him, it was making him crazy. The rope was thick and heavy to handle. If only people knew why. The options played around his head like a broken record. He was the reason his family were dead. They were gone forever, and this killed him. Gone...

Nikita Goulding (13)
Unity College, Towneley Holmes

THE MADWOMAN

She'd always had an awful reputation, talking to herself, everyone thought she was mad. Lingering at the graveyard, she stands, an isolated figure. Who was she talking to? Someone or something?

To the locals, she was the madwoman - but she wasn't mad at all. Who was she muttering to? Well, who wasn't she muttering to? Strangely, she possessed a rare supernatural gift where she could communicate with the deceased. Judging her, the living always questioned why she was at the graveyard. Little did they know, she would talk to them once they passed away.

Jenson Thomas (14)
Unity College, Towneley Holmes

THE GRAVE

The thick, heavy trees swayed back and forth in the wind. Fiercely, the rain hit the cobblestone path leading to the graveyard. The rain hit the old gravestone sitting there in the soil. A figure with a hunched back was getting drenched in her precious button-up coat.

Her glasses steamed up from the heavy rain. Intensely staring at her husband's grave, remorse started to cloud up her head. "Why?" she said to herself in a sad tone. "Why did you have to go?" she yelled in anger. Repeating those words in her head, Helena started to leave.

Courtenay Gallagher-Knowles (14)
Unity College, Towneley Holmes

HAUNTED

Finally, I was about to win. One more spook would force them out of my treasured house. They took everything from me, even killed me, and they still thought I'd be okay with them. Well, I wasn't!

I concentrated my enchantments into one place and cast my most powerful charm into the night sky. All was silent until a blaring scream shattered the dense atmosphere. The friends of my former life were terrified.

It felt great to be back in control of my childhood manor. My troubles were over. I was finally free from the chains I was trapped with.

Jessica Cullivan (13)
Unity College, Towneley Holmes

ELIZABETH

In the piercing coldness of the graveyard. Elizabeth remembered all the fun times with her husband and son. All the meals around the table. But she came to the realisation that her family had been destroyed. It was all down to her. Elizabeth stood alone, hearing voices all around her. Feeling trapped and isolated. Suddenly, the evil side to her came out and was waiting for her next victim, like a lion waiting for its prey.

Then, when she turned around, two graves started opening. Waiting for the people to be seen, who they were will never be known.

Evie Whitehead (13)
Unity College, Towneley Holmes

MY GREAT ESCAPE

The plan was in motion. The bomb I'd planted was about to explode, bringing the enemy operation down with it. All I had to do now was escape. Left, right, then right again. I was lost.

No, this can't be happening, I thought to myself as I raced down the halls. *This way? I can't remember.* I had one minute to get out of there before the building exploded with me inside.

I sprinted, looking for a way out. Fortunately, I found a window. I jumped out onto a pile of leaves in the shining daylight, grateful for my life.

Grace Hargreaves (14)
Unity College, Towneley Holmes

DO NOT DISTURB

She stared at the neglected stone in front of her. The cold rain was pelting down around her. She seemed to keep all her attention on the gravestone, still cautious of the distant sounds from the nearby town.

Suddenly, the sounds began to get louder until she felt as if someone was breathing down her neck. She spun around and took a sharp breath, how dare anyone disturb her peace!

She grabbed the boy by his neck and crushed his windpipe until his face went discoloured and his frail body finally went limp. She didn't like being disturbed.

Lacey Laycock (13)

Unity College, Towneley Holmes

FINALLY

Fog loomed over the valley while the rain poured on the forest below. She peered at the cold stone in front of her. "I miss you," she muttered as tears dripped down her face. Behind a tree in the distance, a dark silhouette appeared. His eyes glared at her as if he was after something. Within a few seconds, he'd gone.

Slash! The knife ruptured her skin and blood oozed out of her body, creating a dark, red puddle on the floor. Her lifeless body dropped onto the floor. Leaning over her, he pulled the bloody knife out.

Ellie Romao (14)
Unity College, Towneley Holmes

THE START OF SOMETHING NEW

Alarms blared, stopping Leo from wedging money into his duffel bag. A click from his right caught his attention. Leo's breath caught in his throat and his eyes widened. His dad. What was he doing? They were meant to be on the same side! It was a trap.

Something within Leo snapped. A burning passion for his dad arose. Too fast for his dad to comprehend, Leo seized the gun out of his hand, aiming at his dad. *Bang!* He tumbled down as Leo chuckled sinisterly.

Men with guns blazed in on high alert. He was surrounded. It was over.

Aliceya Conroy (13)
Unity College, Towneley Holmes

THE HURT WOMAN

After the horrible death of Juliet (the hurt woman) the house she lived in became open to the public, where people could spend the night. One of the people booked for the night was the murderer of Juliet. Nobody knew it was him, except for the hurt woman's spirit.

He started to explore the house but when the clock chimed 3am, he heard a noise from the music room. He entered the room, suddenly, the door locked behind him and the room was immersed in darkness. Something brushed on his back. He slowly turned around, pale faced. It was her.

Lacey Egerton (13)
Unity College, Towneley Holmes

I HATE SOCIETY

I never really belonged in society after that day. After my face was destroyed. Family, friends, lovers, all pushed away. Chris Harris, the guy that ruined my life, was now dead. Well, you might be thinking what brought me to this. It was 2009. He robbed me, stabbed me, and left me in the cold, dark, rainy street. He thought I was dead. He left me to die. I tried to talk to my friends, they wouldn't help me. Neither would my family. And that's why I killed him. My 'friends' were next. And that was why I hated society.

Taiyan Burke (13)
Unity College, Towneley Holmes

ZOMBIE APOCALYPSE

I did it to survive. Seven years ago, a zombie apocalypse started. Me and my brother were walking down to our nearest zombie-infested town, to see if we could scavenge any supplies. Instead, we found ourselves cornered by zombies.

I was at a metal gate we could close. My brother was running as fast as he could to reach the door but they were gaining on him too fast and would get through if I didn't close the door. Regretting my decisions, I did it. I watched, horrified, as I saw my brother being ripped apart and screaming in agony.

Jake Kostilek (13)
Unity College, Towneley Holmes

THE WAILING FOREST

Trees fell like a chain of dominos, one after one. Lightning struck, no rain followed. Wildly, the wind whistled and churned. Although the woman stood like a statue. Loud screams screeched out from the forest in the darkness. Silently, the woman still stood, as if she was frozen. Rapidly, a towering tree that had stood for years tumbled toward the - what appeared to be human. But she still stood there. Not even a flinch. *Crash!* Two minutes later, there was no movement until she walked away. Unscared as if nothing had happened.

Myles Blakey (13)
Unity College, Towneley Holmes

MR NORMAN

The wind cried, just like Mr Norman haunting his son's grave. His heart beaten and broken because of the curse inflicted on him. The wind crashed against his face but he didn't flinch. It seemed he had gotten used to it.

How long had he been here? How old was he? Was he dead? Children used to sing songs about Mr Norman. The song mentioned that he was looking for a child to sacrifice to bring his child back.

He had been standing there for years, feasting on children and waiting for the right child to be the best sacrifice.

Liam Shaw (14)
Unity College, Towneley Holmes

MEDUSA

She used to be beautiful but she had betrayed her beloved, Zeus. One of the most mighty gods, of lightning and thunder. For payback of what Medusa had done, Zeus turned her into a snake-head. The most evil curse. For the rest of eternity.

She does not agree and doesn't like the snakes. She doesn't want to be like this, nor turn people to solid stone. Her slitheringly sly snakes hissing and whispering loudly non-stop inside her head, trying to get her to join the plan of turning everyone to stone. Nothing will ever be the same.

William Lord (13)
Unity College, Towneley Holmes

DEAD OR ALIVE?

On a cold, mysterious night, an ugly character stood in a graveyard. Crashing, booming wind and rain. Reminiscing thoughts in her mind. Thinking about all the brilliant times she used to have.

As she was so worried, she swooshed underground to visit her sister. Dragged by the wild weather, worried she might be stuck, very unexpected. She liked to explore all the dead bodies, almost like a ghost. This hag hobbled through the graveyard, searching through the flesh and bones. Never knowing, was she dead or alive? No soul would ever know.

Eva-Mai Morgan (13)
Unity College, Towneley Holmes

A DAY IN MID-WINTER

I never really belonged with other people. I didn't like school, I liked being alone and I wanted that to be the case. It was mid-winter when it happened. Rainy and dark.

I don't regret it. He wouldn't leave me alone. I took out a pocket knife and stabbed him in the chest over and over. Screams and wails filled the street as the rain pounded onto the concrete.

I waited for the police to arrive. I wanted to see the look on their faces. They arrested me very swiftly and then my wide smile broke into a demonic laugh.

Owen Harris (13)
Unity College, Towneley Holmes

THE WALK-IN WARDROBE

It was a dull morning and a house in the middle of nowhere had been bought. There were warning signs surrounding the perimeter but they didn't bother the new owners.
A day later, they were filling the house with furniture when they came across a wardrobe. Not just any wardrobe but an ancient, walk-in wardrobe. In the wardrobe was a shoebox with a note that said: *Go away, leave us in peace.* Strangely, in the wardrobe, there was a hidden path leading to another room where a family of four lay dead, in peace, in silence.

Bailey Canby (14)
Unity College, Towneley Holmes

REVENGE

Silently, she stared at the shiny gravestone in front of her. She smiled to her family who were stood behind her. They gave her a small smile. They felt sorry for her. She wanted them to feel remorse, she needed them to.

When they were out of sight, she wiped her tears away. Pulling off her wedding band, the side of her mouth curled into a smile. She dabbed at her face and threw the ring on the ground, losing it in the weeds.

"Revenge for taking my son." With that, she walked away through the tall trees with rage.

Rowanne May-Jones (13)
Unity College, Towneley Holmes

THE CHILD

One cold, howling night, there was this woman who was dressed in black. She was skinny, muddy, smelly. She was miserable. Her face was wrinkly, eyes black as darkness. She used to have a beautiful life. Husband, child, and a good job. However she wasn't nice to her son, so he was taken away from her. She became furious and lashed out at people in society, blaming them for her child's death. She retaliated by killing other children and making their parents suffer the way she had. However, she died a couple of weeks later.

Jack Butter-Haworth
Unity College, Towneley Holmes

VECTOR

Once upon a time, there was a guy called Vector. He was evil and scared people. There was a little boy and the boy was eight years old. When Vector found out about the little boy, he went to him when he was sleeping. Vector was whispering, "I am going to follow you everywhere you go." When the little boy woke up, he was scared because he wasn't even sleeping. Before his mum died, she said there was an evil guy called Vector. He went to his mum and said, "I am being followed, but don't worry, Mum."

Bedianur Sahin (11)

Unity College, Towneley Holmes

THE VENGEFUL GHOST

I never really belonged in the neighbourhood. I wanted to haunt every person that'd hurt me in the past. Even if I haunted them, my daughter would not come back.
I wasn't always like this. Evil. Cruel. Revengeful. All I wanted was more justice. That's it. I was actually really glad my plan was going in motion. There was a problem though - my daughter would not be able to come back alive. That made me heartbroken. Very. I killed people, threatened them, and haunted them. I did this for my justice. My own justice.

Khadijah Sarwar (14)
Unity College, Towneley Holmes

BATTLE WITH DARKNESS

Rain pelted the roof and wind lashed the walls of the hospital. Yet no weather could compare to the monster I was battling. The wind howled like the evil cackle of the beast.

I drew my sword, held my shield close to my chest. I didn't blink, didn't move, I didn't flinch. My gaze never broke away from the monster that was trying to take over me. It lashed out a claw at my face and the darkness began to grow stronger.

No man or woman could defeat the darkness. The only option was to surrender. The beast won.

Shaania Alicia Shaw-Miah (13)

Unity College, Towneley Holmes

THE FIGURE

As the rain poured down, I heard screams of my name. It felt like screeching through my ears. As I got closer and closer to the abandoned shack in the woods, a deathly figure glared right at me. Piercing red eyes, black hair, and a skinny, pale body stood in the doorway with a terrifying smile.

Turning around in mystery, like she wanted me to follow, I saw red stains all over the walls and floors. It smelt as if something was rotting. In the corner of the room, beneath the dark shadows, a little girl's body decayed.

Tegan Dowling (14)
Unity College, Towneley Holmes

THE TIME A NEW DEATH AWOKE

The world we live in had the motivation to kill. As a young child, even I didn't want to kill. My world was full of deranged psychosis. I remembered getting chased by this really unhinged man carrying an axe. He caught up to me. That was when Death appeared. He was just a floating black cloud with red eyes, filled with people's deepest desires. That was when he made me his assistant. He trained me to become Death when he retired. So that is how I became Death and how I was looking for revenge on those filthy psychos.

Alex Hughes (13)

Unity College, Towneley Holmes

MY VICTORY

As we both sat in that cave, in awkward silence, I pondered over my failure. The battle was lost, but I dragged him down with me. I stared up at the stars in the gloaming. I unsheathed my dagger and placed it by my thigh. I paused. "You know, I've enjoyed all this," I muttered, a smirk on my face.

He turned and glared. Seething after all I'd done to him, he lunged at me and began to wrap his hands around my throat. I plunged my dagger into his side and revelled in my victory - I'd killed him.

Haaris Yaqub (15)
Unity College, Towneley Holmes

THE WRONG PERSON

I heard a noise coming from the back room. As I walked over to the old oak door, I could hear my heartbeat in my chest. The handle creaked as I turned it nervously. All that was going through my mind was, *what is behind this door?* When I opened the door, they were all there. All of my 'victims'. Their faces full of anger while I was full of fear. They began to crowd around me but they didn't speak, just stared. I noticed a few of them had weapons. If only people knew, they were the real villains.

Lottie Norwood (13)
Unity College, Towneley Holmes

A SOUL IN THE WOODS

Sat in the woods, was a tombstone. The name written on it was James Quell. James had fought in World War 1 for the British Army and was a brave soldier fighting the Germans. After the war, James lived a peaceful life with his wife and young son. Then, suddenly one day, a robber broke into his house and savagely killed his beloved family. James went to look for the robber to seek revenge but was also brutally murdered. His dead body was taken to a forest and buried - where, wanting vengeance, his soul was at unrest.

Isaac Ingham (13)
Unity College, Towneley Holmes

THE WINDOW CLEANER

I'm here to tell the tale of heartbreak and betrayal. Of a girl, once was so bright until that one fateful night. When the boy she loved so much, broke her heart with just one touch. Her love, she thought, would never go, but he fell out of her window. He landed on her greatest friend, now love and friendship met its end. On the pavement outside her front door there really was some blood and gore. The anger and the turmoil, each day would really beat her. She vanquished all her demons and killed the window cleaner.

Emily Haworth (12)

Unity College, Towneley Holmes

THE HOUSE

Bang! Bang! Bang! The woman knocked on the door. No response. The woman knocked again, still no response. She took a step forward, about to head home, until she heard the door quietly open. She turned around, no one was there. "Hello?" She walked toward the door. "Hello?" she called out again. The woman took a step inside the house, and another. The door closed. She gasped in shock. The curtains moved in the rhythm of the wind. The woman was never seen again from that day onward.

Destiny Mannan
Unity College, Towneley Holmes

A HEROIC VILLAIN

There was a superhero who had a power that everyone was shocked by. He had something inside him that people would kill for. A power where he knew who was, deep down, a bad person. He would go and kill bad people.

Every day there was a new killing on the news. It was him! Every night he would go out and kill a new person. He was sentenced to go to jail - until something didn't add up. All the people that he'd killed had very bad criminal records. Maybe he wasn't a villain after all, but a hero.

Alfie Johnson (13)

Unity College, Towneley Holmes

WAITING

She stands in the cold, holding a rose. Crying, she puts the rose on her mother's gravestone and leaves. As she is walking, she can't help but recall her past. That day, she came home to find her mother dead on the floor. The immense pain she felt suddenly turns to anger.
Enraged by the thoughts, she picks up a knife and goes on a killing spree, killing anyone in her way. But, as she is about to kill a child, she realises what she's done. So she hides in the graveyard, watching and waiting.

Ethan Turnbull (13)
Unity College, Towneley Holmes

NOT MY FAULT

I never really belonged. Kidnapped at the age of ten. Taught to behave in that monstrous way. I could never do it again. The only reason I did it was to survive. Who knows what he would have done if I disobeyed?

Actually, I know. He would've murdered me, in the most painful and horrendous way you could ever imagine. The same way I was forced to kill her.

Most people see me as a villain. Some will see me as an evil monster. But no one will see the sweet, innocent boy who was torn from reality.

Amelia Dean (14)
Unity College, Towneley Holmes

AN EYE FOR AN EYE

I had to make up for what I'd done because, one day, my mother was fighting a superhero. I walked up to my mother which caused her to take her eyes off the superhero, which caused her to die because she got killed by the superhero who was granted the power of controlling fire.

Ever since then, I had been killing everyone who reminds me of the hero. Until I came across a man who had the exact facial features. I crept toward them. When I reached them, I was extremely sure it was him. Or was it not?

Owen Sharples (14)
Unity College, Towneley Holmes

BURNLEY BOY

It was a late night down in Burnley and Sour was out, hunting for bad people to kill. Sour was a strange-looking man but was normal on the inside. He had a bald, lumpy head and always wore a Burnley shirt.

Once, two men were fighting and he killed them both, thinking he was a hero - but that wasn't a first. He did it daily, thinking he was a hero and that he'd done the right thing. He once got attacked by a young gang but only one person got out alive and that person was Sour, the villain.

Jaxon Ryder Cole (14)
Unity College, Towneley Holmes

THE BROKEN GIRL

I did it to survive. I grabbed the nearest thing and smashed it over her head. In panic, I realised what I'd done. She'd hurt me really badly. Everyone saw me as the bad person but it was only self-defence. I did everyone a favour by killing her before she did it to someone else.

I know what I did was wrong but I was only protecting myself. I stood in the dock, waiting to see if I was found guilty or not. I started to sweat. My stomach was in knots. I wasn't who they thought I was.

Lola-Boe Robinson (14)

Unity College, Towneley Holmes

THE MAN

The other day, I was in my house and I saw a man standing outside it! At first, he was just coming some days but then he started appearing twice a day, even three times. Just out of the blue, once before I went to sleep he appeared! It got to the point where I had to tell the police. When I rang them, they said that they would come and do some checks. Surprise, surprise, he didn't turn up until they were gone! I took matters into my own hands. It's okay! He's gone now, forever and ever.

Evie Preston (13)
Unity College, Towneley Holmes

RUSTLING

I could hear my heart thudding in my chest as I ran through the trees. Curious, I peered behind me to catch a glimpse of it. I could hear it rustling in the leaves. Quickly, I turned away and ran faster.

I began to run out of breath, I needed somewhere to hide, somewhere safe. In the distance, I could see a cave. With the shred of energy I had left, I trudged through the mud to the cave.

When I finally reached it, I was ready to settle in. Then I saw it and its two, bright piercing eyes.

Annie Fort (14)
Unity College, Towneley Holmes

PURGATORY

She walks alone, in a desolate purgatory. Perfectly trapped between life and death, she is forced to roam for all eternity. Her black, soulless eyes petrify all. Many arrive, few leave. One such victim arrived in her domain, wrapped in curiosity. She fell into the ghoul's gaze and ran in fear. But her fate was sealed. Her sanctuary was a short distance away but the ghoul travelled fast. The adventurer arrived home but felt she had left something. She looked back, her body was face down.

Jasper Cook (13)

Unity College, Towneley Holmes

WAS I REALLY THE VILLAIN?

I never really belonged in fairy tales or myths. I was more on the villain side of things. I still haven't forgotten what they did. The torture they put me through.

My plan had worked. I had finally escaped that dreadful hellhole. I was going to win. I had hatched my final plan. I stood still at the top of the hill, looking down at the mischief I was about to cause in the town below. The revenge I was going to get. After all, they made me turn out this way. Was I really the villain?

Millie-Grace Edmondson (13)
Unity College, Towneley Holmes

VICTORY

I had finally won. Every single hero in sight had been slain.
And I did it. But something about that day felt strange.
Homes abandoned, roads silent. Not a civilian in sight.
I realised what I had done. There was no hero to save them,
so that must have been the reason they left. Was it just me?
Trapped on this desolate, dark Earth. What if something
was coming back my way to get revenge? I knew what I had
to do. I knew it would take a lot of effort - but I needed to
reverse time.

Declan Collinge (13)

Unity College, Towneley Holmes

KNIFE ATTACK

Soft footsteps sounded in the dark bedroom. The dim light of a torch danced across the walls. The footsteps slowed as they came closer to the bed. With great care and without a sound, the torch was placed on the bedside. A bright flash of metal glinted in the torch beam. Arms came up to ward off the flash of light but it did no good. The flashes got harder and faster.

When I woke up, I was in hospital. The doctors had taken my arms and legs. Would I ever survive?

Rajeel Hashmi (14)

Unity College, Towneley Holmes

FLAMES

The cold rain drips onto her pale, emotionless face. She watches the angry flames engulf the house. She smiles happily, knowing her husband is still in the house.
A faint siren appears in the background. She looks down at her hand. A lighter in her hand. The men in black and blue start shouting at her. She can't hear them.
Bang! A loud, eerie gunshot goes off. Her body lies lifeless on the cold, muddy floor. The lighter still in her hand.

Lydia Wrathall (14)
Unity College, Towneley Holmes

THE MAN WHO LOVES HIS KIDS

There she was. The mother of my children. I had always loved her but when she told me I wasn't allowed to see my kids, that was it. She was number one on my list. But first I needed to get my kids back, but how?

I'd kill her. I'd kill her by making sure the kids are at school, then setting her house on fire. The day had come, the day she died. December 30th 1989. The kids had been dropped off at school and Sarah was all alone.

Ruby Milliken (14)
Unity College, Towneley Holmes

YoungWriters®
— Est. 1991 —

YOUNG WRITERS
INFORMATION

We hope you have enjoyed reading this book – and
that you will continue to in the coming years.

If you're a young writer who enjoys reading and creative
writing, or the parent of an enthusiastic poet or story writer,
do visit our website **www.youngwriters.co.uk**. Here you
will find free competitions, workshops and games, as well
as recommended reads, a poetry glossary and our blog.
There's lots to keep budding writers motivated to write!

If you would like to order further copies of this book,
or any of our other titles, then please give us a
call or order via your online account.

Young Writers
Remus House
Coltsfoot Drive
Peterborough
PE2 9BF
(01733) 890066
info@youngwriters.co.uk

Join in the conversation!
Tips, news, giveaways and much more!

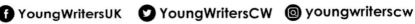
YoungWritersUK   YoungWritersCW   youngwriterscw